W9-BRU-223

The Frozen Face

by
Anne Schraff

Perfection Learning Corporation
Logan, Iowa 51546

Cover Illustration: Michael Aspengren

© 1997 by Perfection Learning Corporation,
1000 North Second Avenue, P.O. Box 500,
Logan, Iowa 51546–0500.
PB ISBN-13: 978-0-7891-1966-7 ISBN-10: 0-7891-1966-8
RLB ISBN-13: 978-0-7807-6518-4 ISBN-10: 0-7891-6518-

13 14 15 16 17 18 PP 12 11 10 09 08 07

1 LAURA ALLEN HURRIED to the vacant table in the George Washington Carver High School library. She dumped her armload of reference books down with a thud and hoped that the tall stack of books would be enough. Mr. Mason, her Western Civilization teacher, was very demanding, and she wanted to do a good job on the big research paper he expected exactly one week from today.

Laura's hands shook as she opened her notebook. She sat down and stared angrily at her small, trembling hands.

"Why am I such a mouse?" she demanded silently. Other sixteen-year-old girls enjoyed high school. They didn't worry constantly about grades. Laura was a good student. Why couldn't she just relax?

Laura knew that part of her worries were due to her father. Joe Allen was demanding too. He expected his daughter to excel in school—and in everything, for that matter. Laura sometimes felt he expected too much.

"Do your best, Laura, and then some," he'd say. "That's how you go places in this world."

Laura and her father had lived alone for almost a year now. It didn't seem possible to Laura that her mother had been in the hospital in Crescentville that long. But after her mom's breakdown, a hospital seemed to be the only choice.

Laura worried about her mom, alone and so far away. When would she come home? Or would she? The last time Laura had visited her mother she had looked so weak, so vulnerable. Would she ever fully recover? Or was she doomed to spend the rest of her life in hospitals?

And Laura worried about another thing too. Did the constant fear she experienced indicate something? Would *she* fall apart like her mother?

"Hi," said an unfamiliar voice behind her. Laura looked up to see a boy with fine features and wide-set eyes approaching her table. Laura judged he was a sophomore like her, but she'd never seen him at Carver before.

"Hi," Laura said uncertainly.

"I'm Todd," said the smiling boy.

"I'm Laura," Laura said. Meeting new people was another worry Laura had. She never quite knew what to say. Besides, Derek didn't like it when she spoke to other guys.

"I couldn't help noticing you look troubled. Is something wrong?" Todd asked.

Laura was surprised at the question. Why would a stranger be concerned about her?

"Well, I have a paper to write for Western Civilization—on the Middle Ages." Laura nodded toward the stack of books and then glanced around for Derek. "I'm supposed to find examples of poetry about life in that period. But there's just so much information. I'm not sure where to begin."

Todd smiled with an understanding that surprised her. "Here. I've got something that might help you." He opened his book bag and lifted out a huge book. "This is an annotated version of Dante's *Divine Comedy*. You're welcome to borrow it if you'd like."

"Wow," Laura said, "that looks perfect!"

"You can keep it as long as you need it, Laura," Todd offered.

"Thanks! You're a lifesaver!" Laura said. "I was really nervous about finding the right materials."

Suddenly Todd reached out and gently put his hand over Laura's.

"Have no fear," he said, looking straight into Laura's eyes. Then he turned and walked away.

Laura stared after him. How did he know that fear of everything had her tied up in knots most of the time? How could he know?

"Hey, Laura!"

Laura turned to see her best friend, Callie Taylor, weaving her way through the maze of library tables and carrying an armload of books.

"I can't believe Mason's only giving us one week to do this paper," Callie complained, dropping her books next to Laura's and plunking herself down in a chair. "He's such a creep! And what amazes me even more is that you're actually dating his nephew."

"I told you, Callie, Derek's not like his uncle. He's just a little jealous, that's all."

"Whatever you say, girl," said Callie, rolling her eyes.

"Callie," asked Laura, "did you see that guy standing here just now?"

"I didn't see anybody. Who was it?" Callie asked.

"You must have seen him. He was right here a second ago. Wearing a denim shirt? Light brown hair, blue eyes? He said his name was Todd, but I've never seen him before."

Callie shrugged. "Sounds cute. Just my luck, I missed him. What's his last name?"

"I don't know. He didn't say. But, oh, Callie, he gave me goose bumps. He lent me this book for my paper. And just before he left, he put his hand over mine and said, 'Have no fear,' as if he knows how nervous I always am. Who do you suppose he is?"

"Maybe he's new at Carver. Look, Laura, I keep telling you. You've gotta stop being so afraid of everything. You've gotta learn to stand up for yourself—stop letting people push you around."

Easy for you to say, thought Laura. Callie and Laura were opposites. Callie, coffee-skinned and dark-eyed, was bold and outgoing. Pale little Laura was quiet and timid. Callie had an easygoing attitude. Laura worried about everything. Despite their differences, however, the two had been best friends since grade school.

Callie turned her attention to her books. "That Mason! I think he's a sadist. He makes up impossible assignments to torture us." She glanced up and rolled her eyes. "Speaking of sadists—look who's here."

The tall frame of Derek Mason loomed over the girls' table. At six foot six, Derek was a starter on Carver's basketball team, even though he was only a sophomore. He'd been standing in the stacks for a few minutes, and now he pulled up a chair.

"So who's this guy you're talking about, Laura?" he asked. "You maybe got a new boyfriend? Gettin' tired of me?"

Laura felt a chill. She knew Derek was more than "just a little jealous," as she had tried to convince Callie. Laura couldn't even talk to another boy without arousing Derek's suspicion.

"He's just somebody who lent me a book, Derek," she said. But the way Derek looked at her made her feel guilty. He had a way of staring and sort of sneering that made her stomach churn.

"Then why are you shaking?" Derek asked. "Feeling guilty about something?"

"Derek, I never saw that guy before in my life. Honest," Laura protested. But as she spoke, her voice cracked, and she realized how unconvincing she sounded.

Derek reached across the table, taking Laura's small hand in his huge one. "Come on, babe, tell the truth," he said, smiling and yet somehow glaring at the same time.

Callie saw what was happening and snapped, "Leave her alone, you creep. Quit bullying her. Look how upset you've made her." Callie's dark eyes flashed as she continued. "You make me sick, Derek Mason. You're just like that uncle of yours. He flunks kids, and then he laughs about it. You're sadists, both of you."

Laura envied her best friend and

wished she had Callie's spunk. Nobody could scare Callie. But instead, Laura found herself saying, "Honest, Derek. I don't know that boy at all."

"Just make sure it stays that way," Derek said, dropping her hand and standing up.

After Derek was gone, Callie fumed, "Laura! Why do you put up with him? Why don't you just shove a pizza in his face and tell him to drop dead?"

"He's not always that way, Callie," Laura said. It was true. Sometimes Derek could be nice. He was Laura's first real boyfriend. She was so shy that boys never seemed to notice her. But she remembered the day Derek had come up to her in the cafeteria, just as she was sitting down to eat lunch...

"Hey, angel-face," he had said. "Can I sit under your halo?"

Laura had almost fainted when she realized he was speaking to her. He was everything Laura wasn't—sure of himself, outgoing, athletic. On their first date, Derek brought her flowers and took her to a fancy restaurant. For the next month,

Laura was walking on air. But then one day Derek found her talking to one of the other basketball players in the hall. That was when Laura first realized how jealous he was.

"But you've got it all wrong, Derek," Laura had said when he accused her of flirting. "Jamal was just asking me about an assignment."

"Listen, Laura," he had warned, "if you're dating me, you're mine. That means staying away from other guys. Do you hear?"

Laura had nodded her head, too shocked and hurt to protest. But she did what he asked. She avoided speaking to other guys. But she knew Derek had her under his thumb, and she hated herself for it.

Now Laura opened the book Todd had given her and began leafing through the pages.

"Callie, this is going to help me so much!" she said, glancing up at her friend. Just then a movement caught her eye—it was Todd. He was standing in the doorway watching her.

"Callie! Look! There's Todd—by the door," Laura gasped. Callie turned sharply around in her chair and looked to where Laura pointed.

"Where? Where?" she asked. "I don't see anybody!"

2   "HE'S GONE NOW," Laura moaned. "But Callie, you must have seen him. He was right there!"

"I'm sorry, Laura, I didn't see anybody," Callie said.

"I can't believe you didn't see him," Laura cried. Then a thought hit her. "You don't suppose I imagined him, do you? Gosh, Callie, am I losing my mind?"

"That's nonsense, girl," Callie snapped. "The guy gave you the book, didn't he? That's real. I don't see the book disappearing, do you?"

Laura smiled a little as she ran her hand over the embossed cover. "He did give me this book, didn't he? Maybe I'm not crazy."

"I wish someone would give me a book," Callie said. "Mason assigned me art from the Middle Ages. Talk about boring!"

The bell rang, and the girls gathered their books and headed down the crowded hallway. They entered Room 233 and sat down at their desks.

Mr. Mason was standing behind the podium at the front of the room marking the attendance sheet as each student entered. After the bell rang, he addressed the class in his typical manner. "Good afternoon, class," he said with mock cheer.

"Good afternoon, Mr. Mason," a few unenthusiastic voices replied.

"I hope we're all ready for a lively discussion of feudal relationships during the Middle Ages," Mr. Mason said, rubbing his hands together.

A groan arose from the class.

"Oh, come now, people," Mr. Mason said. "Surely you've all read the chapter?"

Laura could tell by his tone that he sensed that many of the students were not prepared.

"In that case," Mr. Mason said, smiling even more broadly, "take out a sheet of paper. We'll have a little pop quiz."

That was just like Mason, Laura thought. Anything to nail those students who hadn't read the chapter. Laura, however, was prepared. She had spent two hours the night before studying the assigned chapter. She breezed through the quiz and hoped to get credit for participation in the discussion that followed. But when she volunteered to answer the questions he asked, Mr. Mason seldom called on her. It was obvious he preferred zeroing in on students who were not prepared. By the end of the period, Laura had a headache. When the bell rang, Mr. Mason left the podium and returned to his desk.

Laura approached his desk and took a deep breath. "Mr. Mason," she asked, "can I find out my grade so far?" Laura knew her father expected her to get an A in Western Civilization.

Mr. Mason flipped through his grade book. "You're doing well enough, Laura. You've got a B+. But you could participate more."

Laura's head throbbed. "I try...I mean, I had my hand up today, but you hardly called on me."

"Oh, I don't think that was the case, Laura," Mr. Mason said. He continued to smile even though his eyes were narrow and cruel. "You're very shy. You rarely participate."

"Mr. Mason, I studied the chapter really hard. I wanted to get credit for participation, so I raised my hand a lot," Laura's voice was tremulous, and she was afraid she was going to cry. But he had to have seen her hand up!

"Are you calling me a liar, Laura?" Mr. Mason asked with a warning in his voice.

"Oh, no, sir," Laura said quickly, "but…"

"End of discussion." Mr. Mason slammed his grade book shut. He rose from his chair and turned to the chalkboard behind him, erasing the writing on the board as if she were no longer there.

Callie was waiting for her in the hall.

"I bet I won't get an A, even though I deserve it," Laura wailed. "And Dad is going to be so mad!"

"Laura, I told you before. You've got to stand up to people—and that includes your father. Talk to your father. Tell him you're doing your best and to back off!" Callie said.

"Oh, I wish I could! But I could never tell my father that. He just doesn't…you know, discuss things. He's not that kind of person."

Callie looked at her watch. "Suit yourself. Oh, I almost forgot. Janine invited us to go ice-skating at Miller's Pond after school. Wanna go?"

"I'd really like to, but I should study," Laura said. "Wait—Dad has to work overtime tonight. The plant got a big order from overseas, and he says they're really scrambling to fill it. Do you think we'd be home by seven?"

"Sure," said her friend.

"Okay, I'll go then."

"Great," said Callie. "The fresh air will do you good. Go home after school and grab your skates. We'll swing by and pick you up."

"Are you driving?" asked Laura.

"No, I can't get the car. Janine's brother is taking us."

It had snowed that week, and the pond was beautiful. The fir trees seemed to be dusted with powdered sugar, and the ice on the pond gleamed in the afternoon sunlight.

"It's so peaceful here," Laura said, lacing up her skates. "I feel like I could stay forever."

"No doubt," said Callie, gliding out onto the ice. "Then I wouldn't have to do that dumb Western Civ. paper."

Callie was very athletic. As she sailed across the ice on one skate, Laura thought she looked almost as good as the Olympic skaters.

"Don't anybody watch me," Laura said. "I usually fall down."

"Here. Let me show you how to hold your body so you don't," Callie said. "It's easy. Just lean forward at your waist like this and push with the front of one blade...short little steps until you feel secure."

"I know," said Laura. "You've shown me that before. But I can never do it."

"Hey, don't sell yourself short, Laura," her friend said. "Give it another try."

Laura hesitated. Then she remembered Todd's words. "Have no fear," he had said. Recalling his soft, strong voice reassured her. She made up her mind. Today she'd go out on the ice and be good. No, great! She'd fly over the ice like Callie, and it would be fun. Oh, how Laura wanted to have fun. How she wanted to forget the pressures and the fears and just have fun!

It was just as well that her dad didn't know she was here. Joe Allen didn't think much of having fun. She remembered the time she'd asked him if she could try out for a small part in the school play. Laura didn't know much about acting, but she thought it looked like fun.

"Fun?" he had barked. "There's plenty of time for fun when you're settled in a job making good money. You just concentrate on getting good grades for now. Fun is the reward that comes when you've paid your dues."

But this wasn't the time to think about her father. Laura was surprised at how well she was skating. As long as she did what Callie showed her and didn't make any sudden moves, she could actually do it! Danny Kerr, Janine's brother, skated past her. "Good going!" he shouted.

Danny was a tall, handsome senior. Laura had admired him from a distance for a long time. But now she blushed from his compliment.

As Janine skated by, she whispered, "My brother thinks you're cute."

"Oh, he's just being nice," Laura said.

Danny caught up with Laura the next time around the pond. "Going to the game Friday?" he asked.

"Yes," Laura said. Derek was playing. He always expected Laura to be there in the stands cheering for him. Or cheering him up after the game if he didn't do well.

"I'm going too," Danny said. "It should be a good game."

"Yeah, it should be," Laura said. She searched for something else to say, but her mind was a blank. That's what always happened when she was around new guys.

"Some of us are going to Jake's Grill afterward. It's a new place. Great burgers and onion rings. Maybe I'll see you there?" Danny said as he skated away.

"Maybe," Laura said. She wished she could go to Jake's. How nice it would be to join a different crowd. But Derek always insisted they go to the Pizza King. That's where the basketball jocks hung out after the game. Besides, even if she talked Derek into going to Jake's, she knew he'd never allow her to associate with another crowd.

It's probably just as well, she thought. She wasn't very good at making impressions, and it wouldn't take Danny or the others long to figure out that she didn't fit in. At least she didn't have to worry about that with Derek.

Laura rounded the next curve with ease. She was glad she'd come. Callie had been right. The fresh air was good for her—cold but invigorating. She wondered how cold it was. Cold enough to freeze the pond beneath her, that was for sure. This ice must be a foot thick, she thought. Laura glanced down. In places the ice seemed almost transparent. So transparent she half expected to see a fish swim by any time.

Suddenly she screamed. There was something beneath the ice! A face! Todd's face! His eyes were open and staring. Blood trickled like frozen threads from the corners of his mouth. Blood was even coming out of his eyes.

She staggered on the ice and fell down. Laura was still screaming when Danny, Janine, and Callie reached her.

"He's down there," she sobbed, "under the ice! He's dead!"

Laura screamed until she thought her head would burst. And then she fainted.

3 WHEN LAURA CAME to, she was lying on the back seat of Danny's car. She saw the concerned faces of Callie and Janine above her.

"You okay, Laura?" Callie asked anxiously. "You passed out!"

Laura remembered Todd's face under the ice. "Who killed Todd?" she groaned, sitting up. "How did he get in the pond?"

"Laura," Janine said with deliberate calm. "I think it was an optical illusion or something. I mean, we all looked, and we didn't see anything in the pond. Nobody's down there. Honest."

"I saw him!" Laura insisted. "I saw Todd. He was bleeding...it was horrible!"

"We all looked," Janine said, "and there was nothing but ice. That pond has been frozen solid for weeks! Callie said you saw that boy at school today. It's not possible that he could be in the pond!"

"You just freaked, Laura," Callie said. "You've been under a lot of pressure lately.

It could happen to anybody."

"Do you want to go to the emergency room?" Danny asked, starting the car.

Laura suddenly remembered her mother talking about things she saw that no one else saw. Was this another similarity between the two of them? Was Laura losing her mind? No, she couldn't be. She wouldn't allow it.

"No, Danny. Really, I'm okay. Just take me home, please," she said finally.

Callie sat next to Laura on the way home. "Laura, really, look what this stress is doing to you. You've got to tell everybody to back off. You have to stand up to your father and to Derek too. Make them stop pressuring you."

"You think I imagined Todd's face in the pond, don't you, Callie?" Laura asked.

Callie hesitated, then said, "Not exactly imagined, Laura. But I think too much stress can cause the mind to do funny things."

"He was there, Callie. I saw him in the pond, and he was murdered," Laura said. "Todd is *dead*!"

"But, Laura, I told you, none of us saw

anything," Callie said as they pulled up to Laura's apartment.

Laura looked for her father's pickup truck. It wasn't in its parking space. Thank goodness he isn't home, she thought. She couldn't face a bunch of questions from him tonight.

"Should I come in and hang out with you for a while, Laura? Like maybe until your dad gets home?" Callie asked.

Laura noted the concern in her voice. She really is a good friend, she thought. I'm lucky to have her.

"No, I'm okay, Callie, really," Laura said as she got out of the car. "But thanks anyway. I'll see you at school tomorrow."

Danny was watching her intently from the front seat. Embarrassed, Laura lowered her eyes. What must he think of her now? A girl who saw dead people in a pond? She gave up any hope of getting to know him better. "Oh…and Danny, thanks for driving," was all she managed to mumble before turning abruptly and hurrying up the sidewalk.

The phone was ringing as she entered the apartment. Probably Derek, she thought, wanting to know where I've been. She threw her books down on the sofa and picked up the receiver.

"Hello?"

An operator said mechanically, "Collect call from Elise Allen. Will you accept the charges?"

Laura froze. It was Mom. Dad left strict orders not to accept her calls. The doctors said it would be better that way. That she shouldn't have too much contact with her family before she had made sufficient progress. That the emotional strain might actually cause her to regress.

"Is that you, Laura?" She could hear her mother pleading on the other end. "Honey, please talk to me!"

Laura knew that both her mother and the operator were waiting for a decision. She took a deep breath.

"I'll accept the call," Laura said.

"Oh, thank you, Laura. I just wanted to hear your voice. How are you, sweetie?"

"I'm fine, Mom," said Laura. It was good to hear her mom's voice too. "How are you doing? Are you okay?"

"Oh, Laura, that's just it. I'm fine. I don't

belong here. You know I don't belong in this place." Her mother sounded like a hurt child. "Some of these people are really sick here. If I stay much longer I'll be just like them."

"I know, Mom. I'm sorry," Laura said softly.

"You're the only one I can turn to, Laura. You have to talk to your father. Make him come here and get me. I'm fine now. All I needed was a rest. You tell him, honey."

"I'll tell him, Mom. I promise," Laura said. "I'd better go now." Laura was afraid her father would walk in any second.

"All right." Her mother sounded disappointed. "I understand. Good-bye, sweetheart. I love you."

"Bye, Mom," Laura said. "Love you too."

* * *

Laura thought back to the night her mother was taken to the hospital. It was the worst night of Laura's life. Elise Allen had always had a sad quality about her, as if something weighed on her mind all the time. But she was a good mother—loving

and caring and warm. Laura was aware
that things between her mother and father
were not so good. Joe Allen was a man of
few words and even fewer emotions.
Rarely did Laura see any signs of affection
between the couple. It was as if something kept them apart, something unseen
but there just the same. Occasionally, late
at night from her bedroom, Laura would
hear her mother trying to talk to her
father in the kitchen.

"Joe," she'd plead. "We have to talk
about it—do something about it. Please.
For my sake. For Laura's sake."

Laura wasn't sure what "it" was, but she
could tell it really bothered her mother.

"Leave it alone, Elise," her father would
say. "What's done is done. It's in the past.
And no amount of talking is going to
change that."

Then her father would turn on the television and refuse to say anything more.
And her mother would go to the bedroom
where Laura could hear her crying softly
through the wall.

Sometimes after such nights, Laura
would ask her mother if there was any-

thing she could do to help.

"No, honey," her mother would say, attempting a weak smile. "There's nothing you can do. There's nothing anyone can do." But despite the smile, Laura could hear the intense sadness in her mother's voice.

Not long before her breakdown, Elise Allen stopped trying to talk to her husband. Laura noticed that the two communicated less and less, sometimes going for days without speaking. But Laura knew something was really wrong when, about a year ago, her mother stopped talking to her. The sadness seemed to turn into a deep depression. She ate very little and seemed to sleep constantly, sometimes for several days at a time. She stopped cooking, and she did the laundry and cleaned the house sporadically. That was when Laura started taking over many of the household duties.

One night Laura came home from school to find her mother huddled in a corner, sobbing. Laura ran to her and knelt beside her.

"Mom, what's wrong?" she asked.

Her mother looked up, eyes flashing with alarm.

"I keep seeing it. Over and over. It never goes away." Her usual quiet voice was wild with fear.

"Seeing what, Mom? What do you keep seeing?"

"He had a gun. He was going to kill us! He said he'd come after us!"

"Mom, what are you talking about? Who had a gun?"

"I can't stand it. I can't stand it anymore!" her mother screamed. And before Laura knew what was happening, Elise Allen dashed across the room to the window. She opened it with a jerk.

"Mom!" Laura cried as cold winter air filled the room. "What are you doing? It's freezing outside. Close the window."

Laura would never forget the look on her mother's face as she turned from the window. It was as if the sadness she had felt all those years had finally become too much to bear, as if she had no choice in what she was about to do.

"I'm sorry, honey," she said. "I truly am sorry."

At that moment, Joe Allen came through the door. "What in the world's going on in here?" he cried. "It's freezing!"

"Dad, stop her!" was all that Laura could yell.

Her father rushed to the window and locked his arms around his wife's waist just as she was scrambling out onto the seventh-story ledge. Back inside, Elise crumpled to the floor, crying. That was when Laura's father had her committed to Mount Mercy Care Center in Crescentville.

Even now Laura's eyes burned with tears as she remembered her mother being led out the door by two paramedics. She hadn't even tried to resist. She simply looked down at the floor and allowed herself to be guided to the elevator.

"Good-bye, Mom," Laura had said tearfully as the elevator doors closed. But her mother hadn't even looked up.

* * *

Joe Allen walked in just as Laura hung up the phone. She tried to wipe away her tears, hoping he wouldn't notice, but it was too late.

"Was that your mother?" he asked.

By not answering, Laura confirmed his suspicions.

"You were talking to your mother when I gave you strict orders not to take any of her calls," he accused.

"She's so desperate, Dad," Laura said. "She wants to come home so badly. She says she feels fine. Hasn't she been there long enough?"

"Laura, your mother's not fine. She may think she is, but she's not. I've talked to the doctors. They say she's made progress, but that it's been slow. If we bring her home too soon, she could have a relapse."

Laura folded quickly. She had been through this too often with her father to think she could win. But every time it happened, she was filled with anger. Why was her mother there in the first place? What had been eating away at her all those years? And why hadn't he talked to her or tried to help her?

Earlier that day, she might have asked her father those questions. "Have no fear," Todd had said. But whether it was real or not, she had seen Todd—dead, under the ice of Miller's Pond. And that experience had shaken Laura and worried her. Why hadn't the others seen him? Did they think she was crazy? Was she? She decided it was best not to mention the incident to her father, so she went into the kitchen and started dinner.

While she worked, Laura listened to the radio. There was no news about Todd. Nothing about finding a dead body beneath the ice at Miller's Pond. Nothing.

As usual, her father said very little at dinner and afterward went to the living room to watch TV. For once, though, Laura was relieved. After the day she'd had, she welcomed the silence. As she was finishing the dishes, Derek called.

"Where were you after school?" he demanded.

"I went ice-skating."

"Where at?"

"Miller's Pond."

"Who with?"

Laura hesitated for only a fraction of a second. "With Callie and Janine," she said, purposely leaving out Danny's name.

But Derek had caught the hesitation in her voice.

"Oh, really? How'd you get there?" He knew that Janine didn't drive and that Callie could rarely get her family's only car.

Laura was suddenly very tired.

"Look, Derek, I've got to do my homework. Can we talk about this tomorrow?"

"All right, babe. But I hope you've got some good answers for me."

The next day at school, a girl Laura hardly knew ran up to her and asked breathlessly, "Did you really see a dead guy in the pond under the ice?"

Laura was shocked. Callie wouldn't say anything to anyone. Either Janine or Danny was spreading it around.

"I don't know what you're talking about," Laura mumbled and quickly walked away.

Danny had been standing nearby in the hall. He came over now, looking apologetic. "Hey, I'm sorry, Laura. My bigmouthed sister happened to tell a couple of her friends. She swore them to secrecy, but you know how that goes. If you get hassled about it, just laugh it off like it was a gag," he said.

He seemed very concerned and very kind. But when she tried to thank him, no sound came out.

Glancing at her watch, Laura hurried to her locker to get her Western Civilization book. Mr. Mason took points off for being late.

Laura yanked out her book and closed her locker. The halls were beginning to clear—a sure sign that the bell was about to ring. Rushing down the hall, she could see a lone figure coming toward her. As she turned into Room 233, she realized who it was.

4 LAURA FROZE IN the doorway and stared down the hall. It was Todd! He wasn't dead! Todd smiled nonchalantly and waved at her. Then he said something. Laura was too far away to hear, but she thought he said, "Gothic." Gothic? Laura repeated to herself. What did he mean by that? As she watched, he disappeared down the next hallway. She took a step to follow him, but the bell started to ring. Quickly she slipped into her seat by the door just as the bell stopped. Mr. Mason glanced up from the podium and said, "See me after class."

Laura was too shocked by what she had just seen to react to Mr. Mason's order. So Todd wasn't dead. Then she couldn't have seen him under the ice. Had it been someone else? But she'd heard nothing about it on the news. Had she imagined it after all?

Laura didn't know whether to be happy or sad. At one point during class, she was able to attract Callie's attention.

"I saw him," she mouthed silently across the room.

"Saw who?" Callie mouthed back.

"Todd."

Callie's eyes widened. "Where?"

"In the hall."

Mr. Mason must have seen the exchange. He suddenly fired a question at Laura.

"Laura!" The sound of her name shot through the room like a bullet over the heads of the other students. "What style of architecture attested to the spirit and vitality of the Middle Ages?"

Laura hesitated, searching frantically in her mind for the answer. Most of the class was watching her.

"We're waiting, Laura," Mr. Mason said.

Suddenly she remembered Todd in the hallway. What had he said?

"Gothic," she blurted out.

He'd done it again—practically saved her life!

Laura noticed that Mr. Mason didn't even acknowledge her answer. He simply turned to another student and asked another question.

When class ended, Laura went up to Mr. Mason's desk.

"You were late, Miss Allen," the teacher said matter-of-factly.

"But I was in my seat before the bell stopped ringing."

"You know the rules in my class. You must be in your seat *before* the bell rings. Do you have an explanation?"

Yes, she thought, but you'd never believe me.

"No, I guess not," she said.

"I've turned your name in to the office," Mr. Mason snapped. "You'll probably be hearing from the attendance secretary. Oh, and I'll also be deducting a few points from the grade book. Good day, Miss Allen." He smiled smugly, turned, and walked out the door.

Miserable, Laura left the room. That was all she needed—to be in trouble with the office. Wait until her dad found out.

Callie was waiting to go to lunch with her.

"Why does that man hate me so much?" Laura asked her friend.

"Mason? He hates everybody," Callie

said. "Don't worry about it. Hey, I can't believe you saw Todd again. That's super!"

"Yeah, I just wish someone else could see him. Let's go to lunch and see if we can spot him."

But in the cafeteria, Derek spoiled any chances of locating Todd. He sat right across from Laura and looked at her in that way he had, smiling and yet sneering at the same time. Laura could only look straight into his eyes or down at the table.

"So how'd you get to Miller's Pond, Laura?" He phrased it as a question, but to Laura it sounded like an accusation.

"Come on, Derek. Give me a break. What difference does it make?"

"None at all. I just want to make sure I can trust you when I'm not around."

"Derek, believe me. I'm not seeing anyone else."

"Is that so? That's not what I heard. I heard you 'saw' somebody—some dead guy under the ice." Derek laughed as he said it. "What's the matter, babe? Am I too hot for you? You looking for someone a little colder—dead cold, maybe?"

Suddenly Laura exploded. Making light

of something that had given her so much pain and worry was going too far.

"How can you say those things?" she cried. "Don't you have any consideration for anyone else?"

Derek looked shocked.

"How do you know I wasn't really upset by what happened? You should be showing some concern instead of making fun of me. All you care about is yourself and whether I'm giving you my undivided attention."

"But, Laura—"

"Well, from now on you won't have to worry. I've had it with your jealousy. I never want to see you again, Derek Mason!"

Callie applauded. "Way to go, Laura!" she shouted. Laura felt a rare rush of pride. She had stood up for herself for the first time in her life. She couldn't imagine what had given her the courage. Yes, she could. It was Todd. Todd, the lifesaver. Todd, the one who had said, "Have no fear."

She walked out of the cafeteria with Callie, leaving Derek at the table with a confused look on his face.

Laura went to the library to work on her paper. She hoped she'd see Todd there again.

"Hey, Laura," Janine said, coming over. "I'm sorry I told my friends about what happened at the pond. I have a hard time keeping my mouth shut. Mom says I'm a motormouth."

Laura shrugged. "It's okay," she said.

"My brother's really mad at me for spilling the beans," Janine said. "He...um...likes you."

Laura said nothing.

"Laura, I just thought I'd tell you. That guy you thought you saw in the pond—Todd? Well, there's nobody by that name registered here at Carver. I checked with the office. We have only one Todd—Todd Carlson, and we've known him since grade school."

"But he gave me a book to help me with my project," Laura said.

"Do you have the book with you?" Janine asked.

"Yes, it's right here in my bag." Laura fished it out and handed it to Janine.

Janine flipped through the pages. "It's an old book. You can tell it's been around for a while. The pages are kind of crumbly. Hey, here's a newspaper clipping. Did you see this, Laura?"

"No," Laura admitted.

"It's an article from the school paper, The Cougar News. Gosh, look at the date—more than twenty years ago! According to this, we had a winning football team back then. That's a switch. Hey, old Mason was the star quarterback. Look at the yellowed picture of him. Boy, he hasn't changed much, has he? Same beady eyes."

"Who's that with him?" Laura asked. "She sure is pretty."

"Looks like the homecoming queen. He seems to be escorting her off the field. I can't read the caption, though. The print's pretty faded."

Laura looked at the picture of Mr. Mason more closely. Janine was right. He hadn't changed much. Same eyes, same smile. He was smiling at the girl on his arm, but he didn't look as if he really liked her. More like he owned her. Laura shuddered. It reminded her of how Derek looked at her.

"Hey, Laura. Let's find some old Carver yearbooks and look him up. It'll be fun to see what else he did in high school. Maybe we can figure out why he's such a jerk now."

"You go ahead, Janine. I've got to get to work." Laura didn't really care what Mr. Mason did in high school. She was more concerned with what he was doing now. Especially as far as her Western Civilization grade was concerned. She turned her attention back to her paper while Janine went to dig up old yearbooks.

A few minutes later, Janine was back.

"Laura, look!" she cried. "I found his senior picture. Jay Mason! What a riot! Look at his hair!" Triumphantly, she held the book open for Laura to see. It was Mason, all right. He looked basically the same except that his hair was longer.

"Let's see what else he did in his senior year," said Janine, sitting down. She consulted the index and then started leafing through the book for pictures of Mr. Mason. Occasionally she paused when something interested her.

"Wow, Laura, look at this guy," she said, pointing at a handsome young man with light brown hair and gentle blue eyes. His picture covered the entire page. "He's so cute." She glanced up at her friend.

"Laura," Janine cried. "What's wrong?"

"Janine!" Laura gasped. "It's him!"

"Who?"

"Todd!" Laura felt weak and dizzy.

"Laura, are you sure?"

"Yes! Or it's a carbon copy of him! But Janine, how can he be in this old yearbook? He's here at Carver now!"

Janine looked closer. "Oh, my gosh! There's a black border around his picture. It says, 'In Memory of Todd Robert Smith—We'll Miss You.' Laura, according to this, he's...dead! And he's been dead for twenty years!"

Laura was past the weakness and the dizziness. Now she simply felt numb all over.

"No...it c-can't be," Laura stammered. "I saw him...in the hall...this morning."

"Oh, Laura, of course it's not him. It couldn't be," Janine said. "Maybe the person you saw was Todd Robert Smith's son."

Laura gently touched the face in the yearbook. It was Todd. She knew it. She didn't want it to be—oh, how she didn't want it to be! But it was. She had seen that face here in the library. She had seen it earlier that day in the hall. And she had seen it under the ice at the pond.

As she lifted her hand from the photograph, she saw blood dripping from her fingertip. She looked down. Blood was running down the picture of Todd's face— at the mouth and the eyes, just like at the pond.

"Janine!" Laura screamed.

5 "LAURA," JANINE CRIED, "you're bleeding! You must have cut yourself on the staple in that old yearbook!"

Laura slammed the book shut and fled from the library. She had to sort things out. Grabbing her coat from her locker, she stepped outside into the cold winter air. The picture had been of Todd. She knew it. But how? And why? Why was she seeing him when no one else was? Why had he come to her? What was the connection between her and a young man who had died twenty years before?

After school Laura stopped off at her Aunt Ellen's. Ellen was her father's younger sister. She had lived in Shady Grove all her life and had attended Carver High. Laura remembered Aunt Ellen talking about her twentieth high school reunion last summer. Maybe Ellen could tell her something about Todd Robert Smith.

Laura decided not to mention the face in the pond. She didn't want to sound like her mother, imagining things. But she did tell Ellen about seeing the memorial to Todd Smith in the yearbook and asked her aunt if she remembered him.

Aunt Ellen looked shocked at Laura's question. She hesitated for some time before finally answering, "Todd Smith, oh yeah. I remember him. I was a freshman just starting at Carver when he was a sophomore. All the freshman girls had a crush on him. He was so nice-looking."

"What happened that he died so young?" Laura asked, afraid of the answer.

Once again Aunt Ellen hesitated. She seemed to be debating something within herself. Finally she shook her head and began slowly.

"It was awful. One Friday night, he disappeared after a basketball game. He wasn't the kind of kid who'd just go off and worry his folks like that. So we all knew something terrible had happened. And sure enough, about five days later, they found him in the pond. It was in the winter—December or January—and there had been some thaws followed by a hard freeze. Some ice fishermen saw his body under the ice. I heard that his eyes were open and there was blood coming out...."

Laura's knuckles were white as she clutched the arm of the chair she was sitting on. "What...what happened to him?" she managed to whisper.

"He'd been shot," Ellen said.

"Shot?" Laura repeated, trembling. "How?"

"The details were really sketchy. The police looked for suspects—someone who might have had a motive. They questioned a few people, but they never found anything substantial. There was some talk that it was suicide. But nobody really knew."

"Suicide?" Laura was shocked.

"Yeah, they thought he might have shot himself at the edge of the pond and then slipped in. The ice had weakened because of the recent thaws. But they never did find the gun. Some people think it's still at the bottom of the pond."

"But why would he kill himself? The way you talked, he had a lot going for himself."

"Nobody ever knew," Aunt Ellen said, shaking her head.

"Well, what do you think, Aunt Ellen? Do you think he committed suicide?"

Aunt Ellen chewed her bottom lip and said, "I don't think so. I think he was murdered."

"Murdered? By whom?"

Ellen sighed deeply. "Look, honey, it doesn't matter what I think. They closed the case years ago. I think you'd better go now. It'll be getting dark soon."

As Laura walked to the bus stop, she thought about what her aunt had said. She was sure now that she'd seen Todd for a reason. She couldn't explain it. There were some things you just couldn't explain. Like soldiers who died in distant battlefields and appeared to their loved ones to say good-bye. Maybe Laura was supposed to be the one to solve Todd's murder. Maybe whoever killed him was still around, a danger to others. But why was she singled out—a girl who was practically afraid of her own shadow?

The phone was ringing when she came in. Laura stared at it miserably. She was sure it was her mom again, pleading to be rescued. She knew she shouldn't accept the call. She could imagine her father's anger if she did.

But Laura loved her. She didn't care what Dad said. She couldn't leave her mother feeling as if nobody cared for her.

"I'll accept the call," Laura told the operator.

"Honey," Mom said in her sad, quiet voice, "did you talk to your father? What did he say about getting me out of here?"

"He said it won't be long now, Mom," Laura lied. She had to give her mother some hope.

"But when, Laura? Can you tell me when? I'm so tired of being here. All I want to do is come home."

"I don't know when for sure, Mom," Laura said. "But I know it'll be soon, real soon."

"When are you coming to see me, Laura? I haven't seen you in so long."

Laura couldn't stand it. Her mother sounded so miserable. She had to see her, to let her know she still loved her. No matter how much her father or the doctors objected.

Laura swallowed hard and said, "This Sunday, Mom. I'm coming this Sunday."

She said it even though she had no idea how she'd get there. It was an hour each way to Crescentville. Maybe Callie could get the family car since it was a Sunday. She'd get there somehow, though. What worried her more was the thought of telling her father. He would want to know where she was going on a Sunday right after church. She knew she should tell him as soon as possible before she had a chance to change her mind.

* * *

"Dad, can I go see Mom this weekend?" she squeaked at dinner.

"Nonsense. It's too soon," her father said without looking up.

"But, Dad," Laura said, trying hard to keep her voice even. "Mom is lonely and scared. She says she really wants to see me. And I want to see her."

Joe Allen breathed a deep sigh. "I know you do, Laura. But I'm only trying to do what's best for her. The doctors say she's improved, but not enough. We just have to give her time—give them time to work with her, to heal her. Do you want to ruin everything they've accomplished?"

Laura stared at her father intently. He was a good man. She never doubted that. He worked hard and provided for his family. But he was a hard man too. She sensed that somewhere deep in his heart, he felt the whole world had let him down, and he was angry. Maybe it was because he had never gone to college. Laura knew that his family had been poor, and college was out of the question. Whatever it was, he had stopped trusting people. He kept a little wall around himself to keep people from getting too close. Never in all the years Laura had known him had he shown much emotion—never had he laughed uncontrollably, or shown affection, or cried. What was it that kept him apart from others? she wondered. What had alienated him from her mother? Well, whatever it was, she wasn't going to allow it to keep her from her mother. She stuck to her guns.

"I'm going to see her, Dad," Laura said firmly.

Joe Allen started to speak but then stood up and left the table, shaking his head. Laura was sorry she'd upset him, but she wouldn't let him affect her decision. He'd been discouraging her from seeing her mother for too long. But what had enabled her to defy him now? she wondered. Then she remembered Todd Smith. She realized he had touched her life in some incredible way. He had given her courage—courage to stand up to Derek and courage to stand up to her father.

Laura owed Todd. And she had to find out who had killed him.

6 "I CAN'T," CALLIE told Laura the next day at school. "I'd really like to, but my mom needs the car on Sunday. I'm sorry."

"That's all right," said Laura. "I'll find another way to get to Crescentville."

"You know," Callie said, "Janine's brother has a car. And he seems to like you. Why don't you call him and ask him to take you? You could offer to pay for the gas."

Laura was surprised at how readily she accepted Callie's suggestion. A few days ago, she wouldn't have dreamed of calling a boy, let alone tell him about her mother's illness. But now, things were different. Now she had the courage, thanks to Todd Smith.

That night she called Danny. He seemed pleased to hear from her. "Sure, Laura, I'll take you." She thought she could hear the smile in his voice.

"You sure you don't mind?" she asked.

"Not at all. In fact, I'm looking forward

to having the chance to talk to you alone for once."

Laura liked Danny. He was nice, and he really did seem to like her.

"Okay, thanks!" she said. "I'll meet you outside my apartment on Sunday about twelve. I go to church with Dad, but we'll be home by then."

The news that Laura was friendly with Danny reached Derek by lunch time the next day. He came over to where Laura and Callie were eating and stood there a few seconds without speaking. Then he said, "So you're hanging out with that jerk, Danny Kerr, huh? What happened to your taste, Laura?"

"I got it back when I stopped dating you," Laura shot back at him.

"Get lost, Derek," Callie snapped. "You're yesterday's news. We already wrapped the garbage in you and tossed it out."

Derek moved closer to Laura and said, "You know that dead guy you saw in Miller's Pond?"

"Don't start with me, Derek," Laura said between clenched teeth.

"Well, I know all about what happened to him," Derek said.

"Liar," Callie said.

"Seriously. I know the whole story, babe. I even know who killed the guy."

"Why don't you tell the police if you know?" Callie demanded.

"Simple. I believe in people minding their own business," Derek said. "The guy who did it is an old man now. He's got a family and a job—you know, a regular respected citizen. No point in stirring up trouble as far as I'm concerned. But I'd tell you, Laura."

"What a liar!" Callie said again. "Look out, Laura. He's just trying to start up with you again."

"I'm serious, babe. I heard it from a reliable source. If you want to hear the whole story, meet me at the Pizza King after school." Leaning even closer to Laura, he said, "It'll freak you out to know who it is. Believe me."

"I don't believe a word you're saying," Laura snapped. "And stop calling me 'babe'."

Derek ignored her. "I guess the guy you

saw—Todd? Was that his name?—was one crazy dude. He didn't like his sister's boyfriend. So when he found them at Miller's Pond together one night, he got in a fight with the guy. The guy killed Todd and put him in the pond."

Laura got up, ignoring Derek. She dumped her trash in a container with a loud thud.

"You're gonna want to know this," Derek said, smiling like a Cheshire cat.

"Leave me alone," Laura said, but she was shaking inside. The story almost sounded plausible.

"Okay, but curiosity's bound to get the best of you, babe. It'll be like an itch you've gotta scratch. You wait and see."

On Saturday Laura did her best to put Derek and his "reliable source" out of her mind. Instead she worked on her Western Civilization paper and looked forward to seeing her mother and Danny the next day.

Sunday finally arrived, and it was cold and beautiful.

As Laura walked home beside her father, he said, "You're making a big mistake, Laura, seeing your mother. You'll get all upset, and your mom will get all upset. It'll only make things worse."

Laura said nothing. She was glad Danny was early. She was glad to get away from the apartment and her father. On the way to Crescentville, Danny didn't ask a lot of questions about her mother's illness, but Laura decided to tell him anyway.

"Mom's always been nervous and kind of weak, and my dad's sort of demanding. Mom needs someone who's...gentle and encouraging. I mean, Dad's a good man and everything, but he doesn't know how to deal with somebody who's...I don't know..."

"Fragile?" Danny supplied the word.

"Yeah, fragile," Laura said, relieved that he hadn't said "crazy" or "loony." But Laura was beginning to realize that Danny wouldn't say anything like that.

"What are the doctors doing for your mom?" he asked.

"They're trying different kinds of medicine. Then, when she's stable, she can come home," Laura said.

"That's good," Danny said, encouragingly. "I had a friend who was really depressed and was in the hospital for a while, but now he's on medication and is doing fine."

As they approached Mount Mercy Care Center, Laura noticed how big and depressing it looked. It always reminded her of a giant ice cube. But inside the walls were a warm yellow, and the furniture was clean and comfortable. Danny waited in the main lobby while Laura went to the visitors' room on her mother's floor.

"Laura!" her mother cried when she saw her.

"Hi, Mom," Laura said, hugging her mother tightly. "Oh, it's so good to see you. You're looking good, Mom." It was true. Her mother did look somewhat better. More rested, at least. But when she looked into her mother's eyes, Laura could tell the old pain was still there.

"Come on. Let's sit over in the corner on the sofa." Her mom led Laura to a secluded place behind some potted plants. Around the room, other patients chatted with their visitors.

"So, how are you, honey?" her mother asked. "You look a little peaked."

"I'm fine, Mom. Just fine," Laura answered in what she hoped was a confident voice. She hadn't realized that the events of the week were taking such an obvious toll on her.

Mrs. Allen narrowed her eyes. "Are you sure? You know I've always been able to tell when something's bothering you."

Oh, Mom, if you only knew, Laura thought. She longed to tell her mother about Todd Smith. About talking to him in the library, then seeing his face in the pond, and finally seeing him in the yearbook. She knew that even if her mother didn't believe her, she would at least have empathy for her. But she couldn't take the chance of upsetting her. So instead she said, "Really, Mom. I'm fine. It's just school—you know, homework and all that."

Her mother looked relieved. "Good. I worry about you, honey. How is school going for you this year?"

"Pretty well."

"Pretty well? You didn't say that with

much enthusiasm. Is your father on your case again?"

"No, really, Dad's okay. But—well, you know Dad."

"Yes, I do," her mother said softly. "But don't let it bother you too much. Joe's a good man. He just doesn't always know how to relate to people very well. But he really is a good man."

Laura and her mother talked for over an hour about little things—the neighborhood, Laura's friends, Aunt Ellen. Although Laura had never told her mom about Derek, she now found herself talking with warm enthusiasm about Danny. Mrs. Allen seemed pleased.

"I'm glad you've found a nice boy, honey."

"Thanks, Mom. I am too. But you haven't told me how you've been."

The old sadness returned to her mother's voice, and suddenly she sounded tired. "That's just it, Laura. Like I told you on the phone, I'm okay now. I'll be the first to admit I needed a rest. But I've had one—a good, long one. And now I'm fine and ready to come back home. Did you talk to your father about my coming home?"

"I did, Mom, and I know it won't be much longer. He told me the doctors say you've improved. Just do me a favor, okay, Mom? Just hang on a little longer. If you really are better, we'll get you out of here soon. Real soon."

When Laura said good-bye to her mother, Mrs. Allen cried a little. But Laura understood. Her mother didn't make a scene or anything, and Laura was glad she'd come.

On the way home, Danny and Laura stopped at the Pizza King. Danny suggested it, and Laura said yes, hoping Derek wouldn't be there on a Sunday afternoon. She was wrong. Derek was there playing pool with some of his friends.

A few minutes after they'd ordered pizza, Derek approached. He tossed a folded piece of paper onto their table and said, "I decided to end the suspense. I wrote the name of the guy who murdered Todd Smith on this piece of paper."

The paper slipped off the table and landed at her feet. Laura tried to ignore both Derek and the paper.

"You'll look at it," Derek said with a chuckle as he walked away.

"What a jerk," Danny said, reaching down to pick up the paper. "Do you want to open it?" he asked.

"No," Laura said. But Derek was right. She was burning with curiosity to see what was written on that paper. Not that she'd believe what Derek had written. But if it got her any closer to figuring out who really had killed Todd Smith, it might be worth it. And maybe Derek did know something. His parents were probably students at Carver around the time Todd was killed. Of course, her parents must have been too. But she didn't know for sure. They rarely spoke about high school. In fact, they rarely spoke about the past at all.

As they ate, Danny attempted to make light conversation, but Laura was distracted by the paper.

"You want to look, don't you?" Danny finally asked.

"I guess so," Laura admitted.

"He's gone now. It wouldn't hurt to look if you want to," Danny said. "You want me to read it and tell you what it says?"

"Please," Laura said.

Danny unfolded the paper. A look of shock crossed his face. Quickly he recovered and said, "It's blank." But he didn't lie very well. Laura snatched the paper from him and read the message, "Your dad did it, babe. Sorry."

7 "LAURA, DON'T LET that stupid lie upset you," Danny urged. "It's just Derek's way of hurting you, of getting back at you for breaking it off with him."

"I know," Laura said. She stuffed the paper in her purse. "I'll burn this as soon as I get home." How could Derek do such a thing? she wondered. It was so hurtful, so hateful. Did he resent her that much?

Danny dropped Laura off at her apartment at five that evening. Her father's truck was there. She dreaded seeing him. Going to visit her mother had been the first time she had really gone against his wishes. She wasn't sure how he'd handle it.

"Hi, Dad," Laura said as she came in.

Joe Allen was sitting in front of the television watching a basketball game. He said, "Hello, Laura," without turning his head.

Laura went into the living room. "Things went great at the hospital today.

Mom looks wonderful. You should have seen her."

No answer.

"Dad, I just wanted to see my mother," Laura sighed. "I'm sorry."

"Never mind, Laura," he said. "What's done is done."

Laura remembered hearing those same words when her mother had tried to talk to him. "What's done is done." Then nothing. The silent treatment. Probably worse than being yelled at. At least if he yelled at her, Laura knew he was noticing her. This way she felt as if he hardly knew she was alive.

"I'll get you some dinner," she said and left him watching the game while she went into the kitchen. She wasn't hungry, but maybe some food would cheer him up. A few minutes later she came in with a plate of food and tried again.

"Dad, really, Mom looks better. Well-rested. And she's got a little color in her cheeks again."

She received a grunt in reply. Her father began eating, never looking away from the television.

His silence frustrated Laura. Maybe her mother was right. Maybe he just didn't know how to relate to people. But Laura felt her father was being cruel by not speaking to her. Finally she could stand it no more.

"Dad, why won't you talk to me?" Laura cried. "You used to do the same thing to Mom—give her the silent treatment until it almost drove her mad. Maybe that's why she's in the hospital. All she needed was someone to talk to about her problems, about whatever it was that was eating away at her. Maybe if you'd have talked to her, she'd still be here today!"

Still no answer.

Laura gave up and went to her room. She tried to do a little homework but had a hard time concentrating. All she could think about was Derek's malicious note. "Your dad did it, babe. Sorry." Ridiculous. He's only trying to hurt me, she thought again. But claiming her father was a murderer was low even for Derek. And he said he'd heard it from a reliable source. Who would be spreading such a thing about her father? And why?

Laura's eyes widened. What if it were true? Her dad had a certain mysteriousness about him. And he was often so withdrawn, so troubled, as if something were weighing on his mind.

What if he had been dating Todd's sister and had made her cry like he made Mom cry? What if Todd's sister had come home from dates an emotional wreck? Maybe Todd couldn't stand to see her suffer like that.

Laura did something she didn't think she'd ever do again. As much as she hated to, she called Derek. She needed to hear his story to see if it rang true.

"I want the truth, Derek," Laura said sharply when he answered the phone. "Not some dirty lie."

"I swear it's true, babe," Derek said. "I told a…friend about your seeing that dead dude in the pond, and he told me all about it. This, um, friend was in high school with Todd Smith."

Laura tried to sound indifferent. "And what did your *friend* say?"

"He said that your dad was dating Todd Smith's sister and was treating her pretty badly. One night Todd found out that they were at Miller's Pond together. So he went out there with a gun to scare your dad away. Instead, your dad got the gun away from him and shot him."

Laura wanted to stop Derek from saying any more, but she couldn't. She had to know the truth.

"And then a few days later a couple of ice fishermen spotted Todd's body. He was staring up through the ice. I guess he had blood coming from his mouth and eyes. Pretty gory, huh?"

Tears streamed down Laura's face. "I don't believe it! My father couldn't have done such a terrible thing!" she cried.

"Suit yourself, babe," Derek said. "But you've told me how your dad is, how he hardly ever talks to you. Maybe something's bothering him—like guilt. Maybe he sees the dude's frozen face in his dreams or something."

"But if he did it, why wasn't he arrested?"

"According to my friend, the police were never able to prove anything because they couldn't find the gun."

"But the girl he was with, Todd Smith's sister—didn't she see it all? Wouldn't she have told the police?"

Derek paused, then said, "I guess she was too scared to talk. Probably afraid of your dad." Then he took a deep breath and said in an odd voice, "You know how your mom's always been."

"My mom? What does she have to do with this?"

"Oh, didn't you know? She was Todd Smith's sister!"

"Wh-what?" Laura stammered. Her knees turned to putty.

"That's right, babe. The guy who's been haunting you? He's your uncle!"

8 LAURA SLAMMED THE phone down, her head spinning. *Her uncle? Todd Smith was her uncle—her mother's brother?* She didn't even know her mother had a brother. She knew her mother's maiden name was Smith, but she'd never connected her mother and Todd. Smith was such a common name, and there was more than one Smith family in Shady Grove. But she still couldn't believe her father had killed Todd. Why would her mother have married him if he had killed her brother?

None of it made any sense. She had to talk to someone. Her mother was out of the question. It would only upset her. And how could she talk to her father if he was the murderer?

Aunt Ellen. Laura remembered how she had hesitated when Laura had asked her about Todd. She knew. She knew everything.

Laura dialed her aunt's number. "Aunt

Ellen, I want to tell you about something that happened to me the other day."

"What's that, honey?" Aunt Ellen asked.

"I went skating out on Miller's Pond, and I had, like, a vision or something."

Aunt Ellen hesitated. "What did you see?"

The words seemed to spill from Laura's mouth. "I saw a dead boy's face under the ice, with blood coming out of his mouth and eyes."

"You saw a face under the ice?" Aunt Ellen asked, obviously shocked.

"Yes. And I found out that his name was Todd Smith and that he died in that pond a long time ago."

Her aunt said nothing.

"Aunt Ellen, I have to ask you this. Was Todd Smith my mother's brother?"

Ellen hesitated, then finally said, "Yes, Laura. He was."

"Why didn't you tell me this before? Why didn't anyone tell me?"

"Laura, I was only trying to protect you. It was a terrible thing. And there were all kinds of rumors going around at the time. I just didn't think you needed to be exposed to that."

Laura took a deep breath. "You said you thought he was murdered. Who do you think killed him, Aunt Ellen?"

Her aunt said nothing.

"Aunt Ellen," Laura said slowly, "was it my father? Did my father kill Todd?"

"Oh, Laura, no. Your father would never do such a thing. He's a good man."

Laura wanted to believe her, but how could she? Aunt Ellen had protected her from the truth earlier. Was her aunt "protecting" her again?

She gave up trying to do her homework or working on her paper due in two days. Instead, she turned out her light and crawled into bed, emotionally exhausted. Through her bedroom door, she could hear muffled voices from the television. It sounded as if her dad was watching the news. A pretty typical thing for a father to do. But how typical was Joe Allen? He was certainly not like Callie's father, outgoing and friendly. He was different—but different enough to be a murderer? Surely her dad couldn't have been harboring such a terrible secret all these years. It was just too horrible to imagine. Laura fell into a troubled sleep, knowing she had to find out the answer but afraid of what she might learn.

In the morning, Laura gulped a glass of orange juice and grabbed a piece of toast to go. She wanted to be out of the apartment before her dad got out of the shower.

She dreaded going to school that morning. For one thing, she didn't have her homework done. But what really bothered her was the thought that it probably wouldn't be long before others at school heard the rumor about her father. She doubted that Derek would be able to keep his mouth shut.

"Where's yours, Miss Allen?" Mr. Mason demanded as everyone but Laura passed their homework forward.

"I didn't do it," Laura answered shortly. A couple of students around her gasped. She was the last person they expected to ignore an assignment and then casually admit it.

"Well, people who don't do their homework get very low grades," Mr. Mason said, making a point of writing something in his grade book.

Who cares?, Laura thought. She was in such turmoil that grades didn't matter any more.

After class, Callie hurried over to Laura. "You okay, girl?" she asked.

Tears instantly filled Laura's eyes. She couldn't even tell Callie, her best friend, about her awful fears. How could she form the words "I think my dad might be a murderer!"

At lunch Laura couldn't eat. She left Callie sitting at the table and went to the most secluded part of the campus, the area behind the library. She sat down on a bench under a tree. What had become of her life, she wondered. Her mother was in a care center with a nervous breakdown. Laura, herself, had seen a ghost. No, not just seen one but spoken to one. She suspected her own father of murder. In the last few days, it seemed as if her world had been turned upside down. How much more could she take? Was she going off the deep end? Was this how her mother had felt right before her breakdown?

Laura went through the rest of the day in a daze. She hurried home, dreading an evening with her father, yet knowing she had to ask him about Todd Smith. When she came in, her father was dozing in front of the TV, so she went into the kitchen and started dinner. As she worked, she wondered how she would approach the subject of Todd Smith. Finally she decided the best way was simply to come right out and ask her father.

Dinner started out quietly, as usual. Laura said little and her father said less. He looked tired.

"Dad," Laura said, gathering up what was left of her courage. "Did you know Mom had a brother?"

Joe Allen jerked his head up from his plate and stared at Laura.

"Who told you that?" he demanded.

"It doesn't matter, Dad. I just found out, that's all. I found out that his name was Todd and that he died a long time ago."

Her father's eyes returned to his plate.

Laura continued. "Why didn't you or Mom ever tell me about him?"

"We thought it best not to," her father mumbled.

"But why, Dad? He was my uncle. I

might have liked knowing about him." Laura heard her father breathe a deep sigh. She sensed she was pushing him.

He glanced up. "I told you, Laura, we thought it best not to. What's done is done. You've found out about him, now let it go, okay?"

"What's done is done." There was that phrase again. Laura ate quietly for a few minutes. Finally she asked, almost whispering, "Dad, how did he die?"

Suddenly, Joe Allen dropped his fork and stood up. Obviously straining to control his anger, he said firmly, "Suicide. He committed suicide. Now drop it, Laura. This conversation is over." He turned abruptly and went into the living room where he switched on the TV.

Laura went to her room in tears. What did her father's reaction mean? The police hadn't ruled Todd's death a definite suicide. How could her father be so certain? Was he lying to cover up his own guilt? Why else would he react so strongly? She felt confused.

Laura picked up the *Divine Comedy* book and began leafing through it, reading a passage here or there. She thought she might as well finish her Western Civilization paper. Anything to get her mind off what was happening.

So much of the poem seemed to be about Dante's courage. Courage to do things he hadn't done before. Courage to face the inevitable. Courage to confront his biggest fears. Perhaps Todd had hoped she'd be inspired by the book.

By the time she finished her paper, it was almost midnight. She was about to turn off her light and go to bed when she heard a strange and terrible sound coming from her father's bedroom.

Laura jumped up and hurried down the hall. Silently, she pushed open the bedroom door. In the dim glow of his bedside lamp, she could see her father sitting in the overstuffed chair in his room, his face in his hands, tears spilling through his big fingers. His shoulders throbbed violently, and deep, shattering sobs rolled from his throat. Having never seen her father cry before, Laura was unsure of what to do. She considered going to him to try to comfort him as she did her mother so often. But she was afraid. She had always been somewhat afraid of her father. Though he'd never struck her, his silence had always held her at bay. And now, in spite of her desperate desire to believe he was innocent, she was more afraid of him than ever.

Laura went back to her bedroom and tried to sleep. She squeezed the pillow over her ears to drown out her father's racking sorrow. Eventually there was silence from his bedroom. Laura fell into a fitful sleep. She dreamed of school and her frustrating efforts to get her Western Civilization paper done. In her dream, she was walking to school, and her papers blew away in a rush of wind. Laura was running in and out of traffic trying to retrieve her report, and Mr. Mason stood on the curb laughing at her. At last she had just one sheet to recover. Mr. Mason stepped squarely on it and looked down at Laura. "Forget it," he said, laughing.

The wild nightmare woke Laura. She crept from her bed and went down the hall to check on her father. Although it was two in the morning, he still sat slumped in the chair, his chin resting on his chest. For a moment Laura was afraid he was dead. Maybe his outpouring of grief—guilt?—had been so wrenching that it had stopped his heart. She had heard of men much younger than her father dying of heart attacks.

Trembling, Laura ventured deeper into the room. She stared at her father's big, round shoulders. Please let him be breathing, she prayed. Please, please, please! Even if he did kill Todd Smith, please let him be alive. It had probably been an accident. He probably didn't intend to. Todd came storming up and found Joe Allen with her mother. It was probably pretty much as Derek told it. A violent fight, and the weaker boy was killed. Laura saw a slight tremor in her father's shoulders and knew he was only sleeping. Relieved, she went back to bed and slept again.

Another nightmare overtook her. She was standing on a hill overlooking Miller's Pond. It was a cold, windy night. The pond was lit by a single floodlight from the adjacent parking lot. She could see the outlines of some people standing on the ice, perhaps skaters. Suddenly, a pickup truck veered into the lot. Todd Smith jumped out carrying something under his arm. Laura could see the flash of gleaming metal as light bounced off the object he carried. Laura groaned, even in her sleep. She wanted to warn him that death awaited him at Miller's Pond. She called out to him, but he couldn't hear her. She was too far away, and the wind was carrying her voice in the opposite direction.

Todd dashed toward the pond. "Elise," he cried, "Elise, I'm here!" From down on the pond, a pretty, frail girl in a light blue sweater screamed. Laura realized it was her mother. Elise Smith screamed and screamed and never really stopped. Laura tossed in her bed. When she opened her eyes, her father stood over her bed—his face unshaven and his clothes rumpled.

9 "YOU WERE HAVING a nightmare. I heard you screaming," her father said thickly. His eyes were bloodshot and slightly swollen.

"I'm sorry," Laura mumbled. Her father turned and left the room. She heard him shower and, a few minutes later, leave for work. Laura ate a little, then put her paper and the *Divine Comedy* book in her bag. Maybe I'll see Todd again, she thought.

In class, she lay the paper on Mr. Mason's desk with the others. She knew she'd done a great job, thanks to Todd and the book, so maybe she'd get a decent grade. Not that she cared much anymore.

At the snack machine, Derek joined her. "How's it going, babe?" he asked.

"Your lie is just about ruining my whole life," Laura snapped.

"It wasn't a lie," Derek insisted. "My source was an eyewitness. He saw the whole thing."

"Yeah, right, Derek," Laura said.

"Look, Laura, if I prove to you I was telling the truth, will you go out with me again?"

The last thing Laura wanted to do was go out with Derek. But she had vowed to find out who murdered Todd Smith.

"What are you getting at?" she asked suspiciously.

"What if I took you to see the eyewitness and let you hear it from him?"

"When?" Laura asked.

"How about right after school? Practice isn't until 4:30 tonight, so I'm free for an hour or so."

Laura hesitated. Again she thought Derek was probably lying. But just on the chance that he wasn't, did she really want to know it? She didn't want to meet anybody who could incriminate her father. But she couldn't stay away from meeting him, either. She couldn't go on living with doubts. She had to know the truth.

"All right, Derek. I'll go."

Derek smiled with satisfaction. "Right after school today, babe. Meet me in the parking lot."

"By the way, who is your source?" Laura asked.

"I can't tell you here. But you'll meet him soon enough, and he'll tell you what he saw," Derek said. "I'll see you right after school."

During eighth period, Laura received a message telling her to report to the office right after school. Oh, great, she thought. The tardy I got in Mr. Mason's class has finally caught up with me.

Luckily, since it was her first tardy of the semester, Laura received only a warning from the attendance secretary. But the procedure took long enough to make her late meeting Derek. Afterwards, she grabbed her book bag and ran to the parking lot.

"It's about time," Derek said when she arrived at his car. "You wanna make me late for practice, babe?"

"I'm sorry, Derek," Laura said. "But I had to report to the office about a tardy *your uncle* gave me."

"Well, hop in. We should still be able to make it, but it'll be cutting it close," Derek said. "Now, you've gotta understand something. The person we're going to see will probably tell you the story as he saw it, but he won't repeat it to the police. He doesn't want to stir up the past, understand?"

"What do you mean, he'll *probably* tell me the story? Didn't he agree to this meeting?"

"Well,…he doesn't exactly know you're coming. But I'm sure it'll be okay. Just remember that he won't talk to the police. He says he figures your father has suffered enough having to live with what he did."

Laura sighed and nodded. She didn't want her father to go to jail. But how could she live with him anymore if what Derek said was true? And how could she not tell the police? Maybe she and Mom could get an apartment together. Laura could get a part-time job. Oh, everything was so uncertain, Laura thought. And she wasn't sure that this meeting would make her life any less confusing.

They drove to a well-kept neighborhood of old Victorian houses with stately oak trees and circular drives. Light snow was falling. At the end of the street, they stopped at an especially ornate house with a huge yard.

"This is it," Derek said, turning into the driveway. "Come on. Let's go in."

Laura picked up her book bag and followed Derek to the door. He rang the bell. When the door opened, Laura gasped. "Mr. Mason!"

Mr. Mason frowned. "What are you doing here?" Then he noticed Derek. "Why did you bring her here?" he demanded.

"She, uh, wants to talk to you…about her father. You know, what happened with that Todd guy…" Laura noticed that even Derek seemed uneasy with his uncle.

Laura broke in. "Mr. Mason, I just want to know the truth. And Derek says you know what happened."

Mr. Mason hesitated, then his manner changed abruptly. He smiled in a pitying way. "Unfortunately, Laura, I do. I saw the whole thing. But are you sure you want to hear it? It's not a pleasant story."

Laura swallowed hard. "Yes," she said, "I have to know."

Mr. Mason motioned the two teenagers

into the house, and then led the way to the living room. Derek and Laura sat on a sofa opposite Mr. Mason.

"Before I tell you this, Laura," Mr. Mason began, "I want you to understand one thing. What your father did was an accident. He and Todd Smith were fighting, as boys will, and tragically, one of them died. That's why I've never gone to the police. It was just an accident. Something that was not planned to happen."

"Just…please…tell me what you saw," Laura said.

"Oh, man!" Derek said suddenly, jumping up from the couch. "Look at the time! I've gotta get to practice. Gosh, Laura, I'm sorry. I didn't realize it was so late." He turned to his uncle. "Uncle Jay, do you think you could take Laura home?"

Laura wasn't sure she liked the idea of riding in a car with her teacher, but she couldn't leave now. She had to get closer to the truth.

"I suppose I could," said Mr. Mason. "I have no plans for the evening. You run along, Derek. I don't want you to be late for practice. You know how upset the coach gets."

"Okay," said Derek. "Thanks, Uncle Jay." He turned to Laura. "And Laura, don't forget the deal we made, okay?"

"Good-bye, Derek," said Laura as Mr. Mason walked him to the front door. A minute later Mason was back.

"All right, Laura, where were we?" said Mr. Mason. "Oh, yes, I was at Miller's Pond that night after the basketball game. A bunch of us were going ice-skating. Anyway, I was the first of my crowd to arrive. When I pulled up, I could see Joe Allen's car parked on the other side of the pond. Your father was there with your mother." Mr. Mason's eyes took on a kind of dreamy look. "Elise was quite something back then. Pretty and outgoing. Everyone liked her. Even I had somewhat of a crush on her, I'll admit."

Laura had a hard time imagining her mother being outgoing. She could only see her mother as quiet and melancholy.

Mr. Mason continued, "I was sitting in my car waiting for the others when I heard a commotion outside. Elise and Joe were arguing. Now this wasn't uncommon. Rumor had it that they argued a lot and that he could be pretty cruel to her. Anyway, I couldn't hear exactly what they were saying, but evidently Elise had been seeing someone else, and Joe was giving her a hard time about it." He hesitated.

"Go on," said Laura quietly. It was easy to imagine her father and mother in such a situation.

"Well, I could hear him yelling at her, something about the fact that he was going after this guy, but first he was going to teach her a lesson. The next thing I know, he grabbed her coat and ran down onto the pond with it. 'Maybe that'll cool off your love for that punk,' he yelled.

"Well, you can imagine. Elise was freezing. It was January. How your father could be that cruel…" Mr. Mason said, shaking his head.

"Elise ran down onto the pond and pleaded with Joe to give her coat back. But he just laughed and held it out of her reach. Just then I saw a pickup truck pull up, and out jumped Elise's brother Todd. And he had a gun. Evidently, he'd heard the rumors about how Joe had been treating Elise, and he tracked them to Miller's Pond that night. I guess he brought his gun to scare Joe into staying away from Elise. I heard him yell, 'Elise, I'm here!'

"He ran down onto the ice and pointed his gun at Joe Allen. 'Give her the coat, Allen!' he shouted. I could see by the floodlight that Joe looked pretty scared. He handed Elise the coat, and she immediately put it on. Then Todd yelled, 'Now, get out of here and leave her alone. Do you hear me, Allen? Don't ever come near my sister again.' Joe made out as if he were turning to walk away, but the next thing I know, he charged into Todd. They struggled for a few minutes, and then the gun went off."

Laura felt sick. Her father was a strong man even now. Back then he was probably even stronger. She remembered Todd standing next to her in the library. He was slightly less than medium height and slender. He probably hadn't stood a chance against her father.

"And then?" Laura whispered.

"Todd was thrown backwards by the

blast. He hit a weak spot in the ice, and it broke beneath him—and he was gone. Just gone.

"And I remember your mother standing there screaming and screaming. I drove as quickly as I could to a pay phone and placed an anonymous call to the police."

Tears slipped down Laura's cheeks. Her mind was spinning wildly, like a carnival ride out of control. Suddenly, she focused on her own nightmare from the other night. In her mind she saw Todd carrying something, something metal. Something gleaming. Something with strings—black shoestrings!

"He didn't have a gun," Laura said quietly, shaking her head.

"Pardon me?" Mr. Mason asked.

"When Todd got out of the car, he was carrying ice skates," Laura said, "not a gun. He came to Miller's Pond to ice-skate."

"Now listen here, Laura, I was there," Mr. Mason protested. "That boy had a gun! He was there to threaten Joe Allen!"

"And my mother didn't have a coat on," Laura said numbly. "She was standing there in just a sweater, a light blue sweater."

Laura glanced at Mr. Mason. He had a strange look on his face. She continued.

"She didn't have time to put her coat on. Right after she got her coat back, Todd was shot. And she started screaming." Laura's heart was pounding so hard she could scarcely breathe. "You don't have your facts straight, Mr. Mason. You're lying!"

"How dare you!" Mason sputtered. "I was there. I saw the whole thing. Joe Allen killed Todd Smith. And it's only through my consideration for your family that I didn't go to the police—that I haven't gone all these years."

"Oh, you were there all right," said Laura. "But it's not because of your kindness that you didn't go to the police. Just who was my mother with that night?" Laura screamed. "You must know that! Was it *you*, Mr. Mason? Was it *you*?"

10 JAY MASON WORKED his mouth in a strange, agitated way. "Okay then—what's the harm in telling you? Elise and I had been dating ever since Homecoming. She was queen that year, and I was king."

Laura suddenly realized the pretty girl in the picture—the one Mr. Mason was looking at as if he owned her—had been her mother.

"But then Joe Allen started hanging around, making a nuisance of himself. He was Todd's best friend, and he'd had a crush on Elise for a long time. He didn't like me. He had never liked me. Once Elise and I started dating, he seemed determined to break us up."

"My father was Todd's best friend?" Laura asked incredulously. Was it true grief then that had caused her father to become withdrawn? Had he been mourning his best friend all these years?

"Yes. And he succeeded in breaking us

up. Between him and Todd, they convinced Elise that I was no good for her. They claimed I was too possessive," Mason said angrily.

"So Elise broke up with me. Right before Christmas! I had a gift for her and everything. Needless to say, I was angry and hurt. She had no right." Mr. Mason said. "But I was determined to get her back. I knew that Friday night Elise and Joe would be at Miller's Pond. They always went ice-skating after the basketball games. What I didn't know was that Todd would join them."

"What *really* happened, Mr. Mason?" Laura demanded.

"I was waiting for them when they got to the pond. I brought my father's pistol along, the one he used for target practice. I planned on scaring Joe Allen away. After all, Elise was mine. I had dated her first. By rights, she belonged to me."

Laura shivered. She could imagine how her mother had felt.

"By a stroke of luck, Elise got there first. Joe was late for some reason. I figured I could approach her alone and convince her to come back to me. I wouldn't even have to use the gun. But she would have nothing to do with me. She told me we were through forever and that she was dating Joe Allen now. They had even discussed marriage. I figured I had to talk some sense into her. She didn't know what was best for her. Joe Allen was from a poor family—he'd never amount to anything. I, on the other hand, was going to college. I had a career planned."

"And taking her coat in the middle of winter was talking some sense into her?" Laura asked bitterly.

"I had to reach her somehow. I had to make her see. So I took her coat and ran down onto the ice with it. I was going to give it back to her. I just wanted to teach her a lesson, that's all. But before I could give it back, Todd pulled up. He didn't see me at first. He called to her, told her he was there, and ran down the hill carrying his skates. But when he got to the pond, he noticed she didn't have a coat on. And then he saw me. He didn't even give me a chance to explain. He just attacked me."

"And you pulled the gun?"

"I had to. He kept hitting me and yelling, 'Leave my sister alone!' I pulled out the gun and told him to get back. He took a step or two back, and then he charged me as hard as he could. We struggled for a few seconds…and the gun went off. He fell backwards. There was a weak spot in the ice. And he was gone. Just like that…gone.

"It was an accident. I didn't mean to kill him. I only wanted to threaten him. Your mother just stood there screaming and screaming. I didn't know what to do. Then Joe Allen came. He heard Elise screaming and saw me with the gun. Then he saw Todd's truck. It didn't take him long to figure out what had happened. But I couldn't have him going to the police. I might have gone to jail. So I told them that if either one of them ever told what had really happened, I would come after them both."

"But the gun?"

"Oh, I still have it. My father left it to me in his will."

"So my father didn't kill Todd Smith—you did! My father wasn't even there when it happened! My mother was your victim, and Todd tried to rescue her, and you killed him!"

"I told you—it was an accident! I didn't mean to kill him!"

"If it was an accident, you should have turned yourself in to the police. Instead, you let my mother and father suffer for years. It was the knowledge of what really happened that caused my mother to have a nervous breakdown. And my father became so guilt-ridden that he couldn't even have a normal relationship with his family. You're despicable, Mr. Mason. You killed Todd, and when Derek told you that I was trying to solve the crime, you thought you could cover up the truth with that monstrous lie about my dad!" Laura ran toward the door. "Well, this lie has come to an end, Mr. Mason. You're finally going to pay for what you did." She grabbed the handle and turned it, but nothing happened. It was locked! She tugged at the door in panic.

"Don't bother, Laura," Mr. Mason hissed. "I locked it when I let Derek out. That's the nice thing about these old houses. You need a key to unlock the door, both inside and out. Unfortunately for you, I have the key. But I'll be unlocking it soon enough."

Laura was terrified. Mr. Mason was drawing nearer, and he had a wild look on his face. "Let me out of here," she screamed. "You'll never get away with this!"

"Oh, that's where you're wrong, Laura," Mr. Mason smiled. "I'm an expert at getting away with things, remember? If you think I'm going to let you ruin me, you're as crazy as your mother." He paused as he reached into a nearby cabinet and pulled out a gun. His tone became threatening. "Now stand back from that door," he ordered.

Laura's gaze darted around in search of an escape route. She ran from the entryway down a corridor. She didn't know where it led, but she was hoping to find a door before Mason caught up to her. The hallway was dark, and she heard him pounding after her. Laura ran faster. Seeing a stairway, she leaped onto the first step, grasped the railing, and flew up the steps, two at a time. Maybe she could dash into an upstairs bedroom, climb out a window onto the roof, and then slide down somewhere.

She reached the top of the stairs and turned down a hallway, veering into the first open room she found. From behind her, she could hear Mr. Mason coming up the stairs. Then she stopped. The only window in the room had an iron grating on the outside!

"Aha," Mason shouted, appearing in the doorway, gun in hand. "Our little bird is trapped in a cage!"

Laura's knees went weak. "Don't shoot me, Mr. Mason. Please don't shoot me!" she cried.

"Oh, don't worry. I'm not going to shoot you—yet! First we have a little trip to take. You know the place, Miller's Pond. We've had a couple of thaws lately, so there won't be any skaters there. The ice should have some pretty weak spots. Why, if I'm lucky, they won't find you until spring!"

Laura's stomach lurched with terror. She stammered, "But Derek...he'll know I was with you. He'll figure it out."

"I doubt it. He's not that smart. Anyway, he knows how distraught you've been. When the police rule it a suicide, it'll make perfect sense to him. And to everyone else. After all, you had an uncle who committed suicide. And you've got a mother in the nuthouse," Mr. Mason gloated. "No, you little pest, you couldn't let sleeping dogs lie. You had to snoop around until you found out who killed your precious uncle. Well, now you're going to have to pay for your little detective work. Downstairs! Now!"

When they reached the living room, Mr. Mason ordered Laura to pick up her book bag. "I don't want any bothersome evidence around," he sneered.

He followed Laura out the front door and into the car, taking care to conceal the gun by pointing it at her through his coat pocket. Laura's mind raced wildly. How could she escape? She decided to run at the first opportunity when they reached the pond. It was her only chance.

It seemed to take only seconds for them to reach their destination. As Laura looked around, she realized that just last week she had thought the pond was a wonderful place, beautiful and isolated. Now it seemed terrifying to her—a place of death.

When they arrived at the parking lot, Mr. Mason got out of the car and headed around to Laura's side. She could see the gun in his hand. She knew what she was about to do was risky, but she had to try. As he opened her door, she pushed on it with all her might, knocking him onto the concrete. Knowing it would not take him long to recover, she instinctively grabbed her bag and headed around to the other side of the car, away from the gun. She could hear him cursing and struggling to his feet. As she looked around frantically, she realized that the only place that offered her any protection was the grove of trees down by the pond. She scrambled down the hill, slipping on the snow as she went.

By the time she reached the trees, Mr. Mason was on his feet and heading down the hill toward her. Just as he entered the grove, Laura ducked behind a huge spruce tree. Through the branches, she could see him stalking, taking care not to step on a twig that would snap or a pine cone that would crunch. She realized by the way he was looking around that he hadn't spotted her location yet. But Laura was more afraid than she had ever been. She had no doubt now that he would kill her. The panic within her was so great that she had to restrain herself from running out from her hiding place and begging for mercy. Maybe if she promised not to tell what she knew, he would believe her and let her live. But even as she thought this, she knew it wasn't so. Mr. Mason had killed once. It might have been an accident, and it might have been a long time ago. But he had killed. And Laura had heard that once a person kills, it's easier the second time. She knew that if she were to survive at all, she would have to keep her head. Be brave. *Have no fear.* She stifled the panic within her and stood perfectly still.

Mr. Mason crept closer, so close that she could hear his heavy breathing. When he reached the spruce tree, he stopped, frowned, and cocked his head slightly, as if listening. Laura knew she had not made a sound. What did he hear?

He began slowly circling the tree. As he moved, so did Laura, keeping just out of his sight around the curve of the tree. She knew he wasn't yet aware of her presence. He was simply searching. But suddenly a twig snapped beneath her foot. She froze. Through the branches a gun appeared. Laura heard Mr. Mason laugh.

"Gotcha!" he said with obvious delight as he appeared. His eyes were gleaming, and his smile was almost demonic. He forced her arm behind her and held the gun to her back.

"Time for a little walk, Laura," he said, steering her toward the pond.

Laura's mind continued to race as they emerged from the trees. What could she do? How could she escape? She had so little time. Be brave, she told herself again. *Have no fear.* The image of Todd—her uncle Todd—appeared in her mind. Gentle eyes, soothing voice. Someone she would have liked to have known. If only he were here now. If only he could help her.

Suddenly Mr. Mason stopped and cocked his head again. "What was that?" he asked.

"I didn't hear anything," Laura stuttered.

"Must be the wind," he said. "Keep moving."

They reached the edge of the pond. Laura looked wildly around, hoping to see someone—anyone who could help her. But the pond was deserted.

Still holding the gun on Laura, Mr. Mason picked up a heavy stick and poked at the ice. It broke fairly easily.

"Just as I thought," he smiled. "It's weak from the thaws, but the weather's supposed to turn cold again—real cold. Guess I'll see you in the spring, Laura."

As he raised the gun, a voice cut through the winter stillness. Mr. Mason turned with a start. Todd Smith was standing on the hill above the pond.

"Laura! Laura, I'm here!" he called, waving his hand.

Mason's eyes grew wide with shock. "Todd Smith? How can that be?" he cried. "He's dead!" He stood unmoving, spellbound by Todd's appearance.

Laura knew this was her chance. As he stared at Todd, she turned suddenly and slammed Mr. Mason in the chest with her book bag. The weight of the bulky *Divine Comedy* book threw him off balance. The gun flew out of his hand and landed in the snow beyond the pond. He staggered and fell, shattering the ice beneath him, and then he disappeared. Laura screamed. Suddenly she felt an arm around her shoulder. Todd was standing beside her.

"Are you all right, Laura?" he asked in his gentle way.

Laura took a deep breath. "I…I'm fine," she said. "Just a little shook up. I'll be okay."

"You were so brave," he said.

"No, not really. Just scared enough to take chances, I guess. I couldn't have done it without you—and Dante. Once again, you saved my life."

She looked at her uncle's light brown hair, blue eyes, and high cheekbones like her mother's. There was a definite family resemblance.

"By now you know who I am, don't you, Laura?" he asked.

She nodded.

"I'm sorry I had to put you through this," Todd went on. "I mean, I'm glad we got a chance to meet. You're everything I'd want in a niece. So like your mother. I only wish I could be here to be a real uncle to you."

Looking at him, it was hard for Laura to believe that this young man could be her uncle. Physically, he was no older than she was. But there was a wisdom about him, an understanding beyond his youthful appearance.

"You realize I can't stay, don't you, Laura?" Todd said.

She nodded again. "But why did you come?" she asked.

"Because the truth had to be told," he answered. "Your parents have suffered for years because of Jay Mason—your mother agonizing over the rumors that I had committed suicide. And your father wracked with guilt over arriving late at the pond. He always felt that if he hadn't been late, he might have saved me. We were best friends, you know."

"But why did you come to me of all people? I've always been such a coward," said Laura.

"No, Laura, you've never been a coward.

Deep down inside you're a very brave person. You just needed someone to tell you so. I knew that if anyone could bring Mason to justice, it would be you."

"What will happen now?" she asked.

"The police will come in a few minutes. I've arranged for that. There's Mason's gun over there. Don't touch it. It's covered with his fingerprints. Tell your story, just as it happened. Tell them everything Jay Mason said about that night. They'll believe you."

"But the police—I'm not sure I can talk to them."

"Of course you can," Todd said gently. "They're just people, Laura, people who want to help you." Then he smiled. "Remember, Laura—have no fear."

"All right, I'll try...but will I see you again?" Laura asked as her eyes filled with tears.

"No, I won't be back. There's no need now. What I've come to do is done, thanks to you. But I'll always be with you, Laura. Right in here, I'll be with you." He pointed toward his heart and smiled. "Good-bye, Laura."

Laura watched as Todd Smith turned and disappeared into the trees.

"Good-bye, Uncle Todd," she said.

She heard a siren approaching and knew the police had arrived. Soon the edge of the pond was swarming with officers. Laura was taken to the police station. Joe Allen was waiting for her when she arrived. He held out his arms, and she ran to him, burying her face in his broad chest.

"Oh, Laura, are you all right?" he asked, tears brimming his eyes. "I was so worried."

"I'm fine, now, Dad," she said. He did love her. She knew that now.

"Excuse me, sir," said one of the officers who had been at the pond, "but we need to question your daughter about what happened. You're welcome to stay."

"Do you want me to, Laura?" asked her father.

"I'd like that very much," she said.

Joe Allen listened as Laura recounted the events of the day. She was careful not to mention anything about seeing Todd. She simply said that Mr. Mason had been distracted by a noise, giving her the opportunity to push him into the pond. The police seemed to accept her story and told her that the pond would be searched for Mr. Mason's body. If everything checked out all right, they would consider the case closed. An article would be placed in the local newspaper telling the truth about what had happened the night Todd Smith died.

"Laura," Joe Allen said on the way home. "I know you had a horrible experience. And I'm sorry it happened to you. But you did something neither your mother nor I had the courage to do all these years. You brought Jay Mason to justice. His threat to kill us kept us from turning him in. I'm very proud of you for your bravery."

"Thanks, Dad," said Laura. "But it must have been awful for you all those years."

"It was, Laura. It was very hard for your mother to live with the rumors that her brother committed suicide. And, of course, I...I lost my best friend." He took a deep breath. "I resented Mason's control but was afraid to say anything. I felt guilty and cowardly all these years. But now that everything's out in the open, I think things will be better, Laura—for all of us."

She thought of her mother, still alone, still in the hospital. Suddenly she missed her more than ever. "Dad? When can I see Mom again?"

Joe Allen looked at his daughter and smiled. "How does tomorrow sound?"

"Do you mean it, Dad? Really?"

"Well, first let's get you home so you can get some rest—you must be exhausted."

"I am," Laura admitted.

"Then tomorrow morning, first thing, we'll go see her. And we'll talk to the doctors. I have a feeling once they find out all that's happened, a lot of your mother's problems will be explained. There may even be a chance that she can come home and just go back for therapy once or twice a week."

"Oh, Dad. That would be wonderful."

"Well, I won't kid you, Laura. It won't be easy. Your mother and I haven't been close for years. I'm not sure how everything will work out. To tell the truth, I find the whole thing kind of scary. "

No, it probably won't be easy, thought

Laura. But the important thing is that he's willing to try.

"I know it must be scary for you, Dad," Laura said, running her fingers over the cover of the *Divine Comedy* book on her lap. She had kept it with her all during the police questioning. It seemed to give her courage. Then Laura did something she'd never done before. She placed her small hand over her father's big hand. It felt right there. And Laura, too, knew that things would be better. "But in the words of someone we both knew and loved, Dad, 'Have no fear'."